Ogres Don't Hunt Easter Eggs

Want more Bailey School Kids?
Check these out!

 #1-46

SUPER SPECIALS #1-6

 #1-10

And don't miss the...

HOLIDAY SPECIALS

Swamp Monsters Don't Chase Wild Turkeys
Aliens Don't Carve Jack-o'-lanterns
Mrs. Claus Doesn't Climb Telephone Poles
Leprechauns Don't Play Fetch
Ogres Don't Hunt Easter Eggs

Ogres Don't Hunt Easter Eggs

by Debbie Dadey
and
Marcia Thornton Jones

illustrated by John Steven Gurney

Scholastic Inc.

New York Toronto London Auckland Sydney
Mexico City New Delhi Hong Kong Buenos Aires

*To Connie Jones, who knows the value of a good
book on a rainy day — and friendship.
— MTJ*

*For the Born family. Thanks for being
such good friends.
— DD*

ISBN-13: 978-0-439-40834-9
ISBN-10: 0-439-40834-2

Text copyright © 2003 by Marcia Thornton Jones and Debra S. Dadey.
Illustrations copyright © 2003 by Scholastic Inc.
All rights reserved. Published by Scholastic Inc. SCHOLASTIC,
LITTLE APPLE, THE ADVENTURES OF THE BAILEY
SCHOOL KIDS, and associated logos are trademarks and/or
registered trademarks of Scholastic Inc.

25 24 23 22 21 20 19 18 17 16 15 14 13   8 9 10 11 12 13/0

Printed in the U.S.A.   40

First printing, March 2003

Contents

1

The Golden Egg

"We're free!" Eddie sang at the top of his lungs. "Free!" He pushed open the door of Bailey Elementary School and raced to the playground. The bell was still ringing when he reached the shade of the giant oak tree. Melody, Liza, and Howie ran after him. Eddie pulled his cap from his red curly hair and flung it in the air.

Liza dodged his cap and let it fall to the ground. "It's not like you don't ever have to go back to school," she said. "We only have a few days off."

"Even a week without school is like a treasure," Eddie said.

Howie lifted his face to the warm sun. "Spring is my favorite time of year," he said, taking a deep breath of fresh air.

1

Overhead, white fluffy clouds floated in a bright blue sky.

Melody bent over and plucked a dandelion from the grass. "Butterflies, sunshine, daffodils. The weather is supposed to be like this all week. What's not to like?"

"This is perfect weather for soccer and racing our bikes down Dedman Hill," Eddie said with a nod.

"And don't forget the Spring Festival in the park," Liza said.

"Who could forget that?" Eddie asked. "It's only the biggest event of the year. I can't wait for the Easter egg hunt. I'm going to find the golden egg this year for sure."

Every year Bailey City had a huge egg hunt. Kids filled baskets with marshmallow bunnies, chocolate ducks, jelly beans, and plastic eggs loaded with candy. But the biggest find of all was the golden egg. With it came a certificate for a grand prize.

"Last year the prize was a bicycle," Liza said.

"The year before that they gave away a trip to Space Camp," Howie said. "I would've given anything to have found the egg that year."

"I wonder what the prize is this year," Melody said.

"Whatever it is, it's bound to be good," Eddie told his friends, "and it's going to be mine. All mine!"

"You don't know that," Melody said with her hands on her hips. "We all have the same chance of finding it."

"Besides," Liza interrupted before Eddie could say another word, "the Easter egg hunt isn't about winning a prize. It's about having fun with your family and friends at the picnic."

Eddie rolled his eyes and kicked his book bag. "I'm not interested in hot dogs and marshmallows. I want to find the golden egg. And to be sure I do, I'm going to the park right now to look for the best hiding places."

Without bothering to wait for his friends, Eddie grabbed his book bag and jogged toward the park. Liza looked at Melody. Melody looked at Howie. Howie shrugged. "It *is* a great day for the park," he said. Then he followed Eddie. Melody and Liza raced after them.

Bumblebees buzzed. A breeze tickled the leaves. Children played on the swing sets. Eddie didn't pay attention to any of those things. Instead, he peeked under benches and behind garbage cans.

"The park is beautiful in the spring," Liza told Melody as they watched Eddie look for hiding places.

Just then, a huge truck missing its muffler lumbered up to the curb and burped to a stop. The back of the truck was filled with plants and shovels and watering buckets. As soon as the door popped open, the sun disappeared beneath a

cloud and thunder growled over Ruby Mountain.

Liza shivered. "It can't rain," she said. "It would ruin the Spring Festival. Nobody wants to hunt for Easter eggs in the rain."

No sooner were the words out of her mouth than a giant man stepped from the truck.

2

Brutus

A huge man with a long hooked nose stood in the shadow of the truck. His shoulders were broad and rounded. He had big ears that stuck straight out from his head along with a few wisps of blond hair. His skin had a green tinge to it. As soon as he noticed the four kids he smiled — only it wasn't much of a smile. The man's thin lip curled up on one side to show a mouthful of crooked, yellow teeth. He rubbed the stubble of whiskers on his chin and looked down at the kids.

"It looks like he's forgotten how to smile," Melody whispered to Liza.

Howie noticed the man's ring on his crooked pinky finger. The man's eyes and the stone in the ring were the exact same color as the gray storm clouds making their way over Ruby Mountain.

Liza cleared her throat and smiled at the man. "Hello," she said. "My name is Liza and these are my friends Howie and Melody. That's Eddie picking up those rocks over there."

The big man glanced at the four kids and grunted. "I'm Brutus," he said in a voice as loud as the thunder. "Brutus Bigg. I've been hired to landscape this park."

Liza clapped her hands. "New flowers and bushes will make the park even prettier."

Howie smiled at Brutus. "You're just in time for the Spring Festival," he said.

Mr. Bigg's crooked smile faded into a grimace. "Spring Festival?" he asked.

Eddie dropped the rock he was holding and nodded. "The whole town comes out for the Spring Festival," he told Mr. Bigg. "This place will be crawling with kids

9

and their parents. They'll all be looking for the golden egg, but I'm the one who's going to find it."

Mr. Bigg glared down at the kids. His eyes narrowed and his face turned a deeper shade of green.

"I hope the weather clears up by then," Melody added quickly, not liking the look on Mr. Bigg's face. "Or else people won't want to come to the park."

Mr. Bigg looked at the sky. He gave his weird little grin again and rubbed the gray stone on his pinky ring. Just then, fat raindrops splattered the ground and lightning flashed in the sky.

"Run!" Liza screamed. "A storm is coming!"

3

The Biggest Pest

"This is horrible," Eddie complained on Tuesday. "I wanted to ride my bike to the park today, but instead I have to hang out in this boring old library. Some vacation this is."

Howie agreed. "It's been miserable all week."

Even Melody looked sad. "It's downright terrible," she muttered. "The weatherman didn't say anything about rain. It's not fair."

"It's only water," Liza said, looking out the window at the rolling gray clouds. "At least the library is open. I've been wanting to get a book on flowers."

Eddie groaned as the four kids went their separate ways in the big Bailey City library. It only took Melody a few minutes to find a new book on soccer. Howie, interested in learning first aid, ended up with a huge book that had a red cross on it.

Liza was checking out her flower book when she wrinkled her nose at a strange earthy smell. Mr. Bigg stood in the doorway of the library. Water dripped off his nearly bald head. He swept his big raincoat off and left it in a puddle on the floor.

"What's he doing here?" Eddie asked, coming up behind Liza.

"He probably wants to find a book," Liza whispered. "Just like us."

"I'm going to follow him," Eddie said. "I'll be just like James Bond, the legendary spy."

Liza rolled her eyes, but Eddie went into sneak mode. He ducked behind stacks of books, dodged around corners, and hid under tables. Mr. Bigg clomped up and down the aisles, his gray eyes scanning the shelves until he spotted the

section where Liza had been looking. "Gardening books," Eddie complained to himself. "They're about as exciting as watching Howie solve a math problem."

Eddie stopped spying and found his friends. "How was your top secret mission?" Melody asked.

"Boring," Eddie said. "The only halfway interesting books Mr. Bigg looked at were the ones on pests."

Liza giggled. "You'd better watch out," she told Eddie. "You're the biggest pest of all!"

"Ha-ha," Eddie said. "You're as funny as

a rotten egg. Now, let's get out of here before I explode from all the excitement."

"You haven't checked out a book yet," Howie said.

"I don't want to read," Eddie griped. "I want to play soccer or run in the park. Better yet, I want to find out what the prize is going to be for finding the golden egg."

"You'll have to settle for finding out what's in a good book," Liza told her friend.

"Fine," Eddie told her. "I'll get a book." He pulled a book from the nearest shelf without even looking at it. The title was *Monsters and Other Giant Tales*.

4

Superspy

"I know what we could do to make this rainy day a little more exciting," Eddie told his friends as they stood on the porch of the library. Rain splashed down around them.

Liza was hoping the rain would let up. She didn't want her books to get wet. "I have to go home soon," she said. "My mom wants me to clean my room today."

Eddie rolled his eyes. "Well, that sounds like fun," he said, without meaning a single word. "But I think we should go on a spying mission to City Hall instead."

"What is it with you and spying?" Melody asked Eddie.

"You'll like this kind of spying," Eddie said with a grin. "Because we'll find out what the grand prize will be at the Easter egg hunt."

Melody smiled before she shook her head. "No way!" she said. "The surprise is part of the fun. They never tell the prize."

"That's why we have to be superspies," Eddie said.

Liza crossed her arms over her chest and held her garden book flat against her body. "It's not nice to snoop."

"But it would be nice to know," Howie admitted.

That's all Eddie needed to hear. He dashed out into the rain. "Last one to City Hall is a hairy monster." Liza, Melody, and Howie hugged their books tight and ran down Smith Avenue after Eddie.

The kids were soaked by the time they got to the porch of the big white building. Liza leaned against one of the columns and squeezed water out of her blond ponytail. "This better be worth getting my book wet," she complained.

"It will be," Eddie said.

Melody sighed. "I hope the prize is a year of free soccer lessons," she said hopefully.

"A year of free candy would be better," Eddie said. "I'd eat it all by myself."

"You won't have any time to play if you win a prize like that," Liza said. "You'll be at the dentist's office every day with cavities."

"I don't care if all the teeth in my head fall out," Eddie said. "I want to win the grand prize."

"Winning isn't everything," Liza reminded Eddie.

"No one will win a thing if the weather doesn't change," Howie said, looking up at the gray clouds. "They'll have to cancel the Spring Festival, including the egg hunt!"

The kids tiptoed into the huge building and sloshed down the hall in their wet shoes. Liza was upset when she saw the muddy mess they left behind them. "I don't think spies leave trails," she whispered to Eddie.

Eddie shrugged as he peeked in different office doors. Melody shivered in her wet clothes. "Let's go home," she said. "This isn't worth catching a cold over."

Eddie didn't answer her. He was creeping into a large office, hunkering down to hide behind desks and chairs.

"What's he doing?" Liza whispered.

"He's hunting for the prize," Howie said, "but he'll get into trouble if he's not careful."

"Aw-choo!" Melody sneezed.

A man in a blue suit stood up from behind a short wall. "Hey," he said. "What are you kids doing in here?"

Eddie stood up from behind a desk and screamed, "Run!"

5

Chicken

"Rain, rain, rain. What kind of vacation is this?" Eddie complained the next day. "Too wet for soccer. Too wet for basketball. Too wet for riding bikes."

Eddie, Melody, Liza, and Howie were at Liza's house. Rain drummed on the roof and streamed down the windows. Eddie plopped on the carpet and sighed.

"Nice weather . . . for ducks," Liza said with a giggle.

"And ogres," Eddie mumbled. "Ogres like rain because they hate people. The rain keeps people from bothering them."

"How do you know that?" Melody asked.

"I've been reading that library book," Eddie admitted. "It's all about monsters."

"Eddie? Reading?" joked Howie. "Quick. Feel his forehead for fever."

Eddie pushed Howie's hand away. "With all this rain, there was nothing else to do."

"Unless you're a pig who likes to play in mud," Melody said with a sigh.

"There's enough mud for ogres in Bailey City," Howie said, looking out the window. "This rain will turn the park into a giant mud pile."

"I hope it stops soon," Melody said, looking out the window. "The Spring Festival is only a few days away. If it keeps raining they'll cancel it for sure."

Eddie jumped up to look out the window. The rain was falling just as hard as before and there was not a single break in the gray clouds. He clenched his fists. "It had better stop raining so I can find the golden egg."

"Don't get your hopes up," Liza warned him. "You might not be the one that finds it."

Eddie sputtered. "I HAVE to win the prize."

"Anyone can win," Melody told him.

"No, they can't," Eddie argued. "Nobody else stands a chance against me."

Melody jutted out her chin and put her hands on her hips. "Don't be so sure," she warned. "I could find that egg just as easily as you."

Eddie glared at Melody. "You could never beat me," Eddie told her.

"Oh yeah?" Melody asked.

"Yeah," Eddie said, stomping his foot on the floor. "I'll prove it at the Spring Festival. I'll find that golden egg so fast it will make your head spin."

"The Spring Festival is three days away. I say we settle this right now," Melody said. "Unless you're chicken."

"The only chicken you'll find around here," Eddie said, "is the one laying Easter eggs!"

6

Something Bad?

"Here's the deal," Eddie said. "We'll hide a bunch of stuff in the park. Whoever finds the most is the winner."

"Okay," Melody said and shook Eddie's hand. "Now, what will we hide?"

"I know!" Liza said, jumping up from the couch. "I have a bag of plastic eggs left over from last year. We can have our very own egg hunt."

Liza rooted through a closet for the eggs. She also found umbrellas for all her friends. She divided the eggs into two piles. "Eddie will hunt for the green eggs. Melody will look for the yellow ones."

Their legs were drenched by the time they reached the park, but they didn't care.

"What happened?" Liza asked as the kids hurried past the Bailey City Park sign.

"It's Mr. Bigg's fault," Eddie said. "He ruined everything."

The park definitely looked different. Mud piles and ditches scarred the play areas. Sidewalks were torn up. Huge rock piles blocked all the entrances.

The kids scrambled around the rocks and jumped over a ditch. "What was he thinking?" Melody asked.

"It's as if Mr. Bigg doesn't want anyone to use the park," Liza said.

"Who would want to, anyway," Howie asked, "in all this rain?"

"I want to," Eddie said, "because I have to show Melody I'm better at hunting Easter eggs. Now let's stop this chitchat and get busy."

The kids divided into two groups to hide the eggs. Howie went with Melody to hide the green eggs. Liza teamed up with Eddie and hid the yellow ones. They wandered through the park, looking for the best hiding places. It didn't take the two teams long before they met back at the picnic shelter.

Howie shook rain from his umbrella and told everyone the rules for the contest. "Liza and Eddie have to look for the green eggs," he said. "Melody and I will look for yellow. You have exactly thirty minutes to search the park."

Eddie was tapping his foot, ready to get moving. He didn't care about rules. He wanted to win. He was just about ready to tell that to Howie when he saw something strange.

"Would you look at that!" Eddie said, interrupting Howie. The kids looked to where Eddie pointed. Mr. Bigg was racing across the park as if his life depended on it.

"Something terrible must be chasing him," Melody said.

"Do you think it's a snake?" Liza asked with a shiver.

"Could be an alligator," Eddie suggested hopefully.

"There are no alligators in Bailey City," Howie told him.

"Whatever it is, it must be bad," Liza said. "Very bad! Do you think we should run, too?"

Mr. Bigg glanced over his shoulder as he ran. His face looked greener than ever and he gasped ragged breaths of air.

"There it is!" Howie said. "I see what's making him run."

7

Puss in Boots

"It's a cat," Liza squealed.

Melody couldn't help giggling. A tiny calico cat was chasing the huge giant of a man. Mr. Bigg ran, his boots smashing dirt clods in his path. The cat, however, was gaining on him. "Mr. Bigg acts as if that cat is a lion."

"A cat scratch *can* hurt," Liza said. "I'd be afraid if a cat chased me, too."

"You're a kid," Melody said. "But Mr. Bigg is a huge man."

"Whoever heard of a giant being afraid of a cat?" Howie said.

Eddie gasped. He gulped. His face turned the color of the clouds overhead.

"Eddie," Liza asked, touching his arm, "are you all right?"

Eddie shook his head, sending rain

spraying from his red hair. "I *do* know about a giant that's afraid of a cat," he said. "The cat in the story *Puss in Boots* tricked an ogre. I read all about it in my library book."

"I still can't believe you're reading a book," Melody said.

"I've read books before," Eddie told Melody, although he couldn't really remember any. "Besides, this one is actually good."

"Maybe I can read it after you," Howie said.

"Then you'll find out how one cat changed ogre history," Eddie told him.

"What are you talking about?" Liza asked.

"According to my book, ogres were once the richest creatures in the world. They could change their shape and they would sneak into villages disguised as coyotes or foxes. Once they were inside they'd turn back into hideous ogres and steal whatever they wanted."

"That's selfish," Liza pointed out.

"The ogres didn't care," Eddie told her.

"They hated people and wanted to be left alone with all the riches they'd stolen. They lived in castles and did whatever they wanted. All that changed when one very tricky cat showed up."

"I would think a cat would be afraid of a giant ogre," Liza said.

"Most were," Eddie said. "But this cat dared the ogre to change into a mouse. And we all know what happens when a mouse comes whisker-to-whisker with a cat."

Liza shuddered. "That poor mouse."

"But lucky for the villagers," Howie pointed out. "The cat saved them from the terrible ogre."

"From that day on, ogres refused to change their shape, and they became deathly afraid of cats. It's true. It has to be. I read it." Suddenly Eddie stumbled until his back was flat against soggy tree bark. "Holy Toledo," he gasped. "I know why Mr. Bigg is here!"

Liza nodded. "He's fixing up the park." But then she giggled. "Actually right now he's running from a cat. Maybe we should help him." The kids watched as Mr. Bigg dodged a park bench. The cat hopped on the bench and scrambled over the back. It jumped right in front of the running man. Mr. Bigg skidded to the left, darted around a tree, and headed toward the park entrance.

"No," Eddie said. "We definitely shouldn't help him and I'll tell you why. Mr. Bigg likes dirt and mud. He's messed up the park so no one will come here and bother him. And we all know he's afraid of cats. That can only mean one thing."

"What?" Howie asked.

"Mr. Bigg is an ogre," Eddie said with a gulp. "And he's come to claim our park as his home!"

Liza smiled at the thought of an ogre in their park, but Melody laughed out loud. Even Howie snickered a bit. Eddie did not like to be laughed at. His face

turned bright red and he stomped off through a mud puddle.

"Wait," Liza called after Eddie. "We didn't mean to laugh at you." Liza, Melody, and Howie rushed after Eddie.

Eddie didn't slow down. He stomped through every mud puddle in his path and climbed over big chunks of broken concrete.

Eddie, Melody, Liza, and Howie made their way toward the street entrance. Eddie ran around a giant pile of concrete and stopped. Melody, Liza, and Howie bumped into him.

"I can't believe it!" Liza squealed.

8

Rotten Eggs

"He has our eggs," Eddie snapped as the kids walked toward Mr. Bigg. A car zipped by, spraying all four kids with muddy water.

Mr. Bigg was breathing hard from his race across the park, but the cat was nowhere to be seen.

"Do you think he hurt the cat?" Liza worried.

Melody shook her head. "I'm sure the cat ran away because of the traffic."

"We didn't even have a chance to hunt for the eggs," Melody complained. "He ruined our contest. Now we'll never know who the best spy is."

The four kids stared at Mr. Bigg. He was near the entrance to the park and he held a huge Easter basket in his right hand. The basket was filled with plastic eggs.

"How did Mr. Bigg find the eggs so fast?" Liza asked.

"And what is he going to do with them?" Howie wondered.

"Maybe he wanted to have his own egg hunt," Melody teased.

Liza walked toward Mr. Bigg. "We'll just explain to him that those eggs belong to us," she said, but she stopped short when Mr. Bigg tossed all of the eggs and the basket into the trash can. He wiped his hands on his pants and stomped away.

"Hey, he can't do that," Melody said.

"He just did," Eddie told Melody.

"That's rotten," Howie said.

"As in rotten eggs," Eddie chimed in.

"You'd think Mr. Bigg doesn't want anyone to have fun," Melody said. She held her umbrella over her head and pouted.

"He doesn't," Eddie told his friends.

"Ogres don't like people and they love rain and mud. That's why he's turning our park into the biggest mud pit this side of the Mississippi."

Liza's eyes grew wide. "You mean Mr. Bigg brought this rain with him?"

Howie gasped. "Did you see that ring he wears?" he asked. "It's the exact same color as the clouds and as soon as he rubbed it, rain poured down. It must be magic."

Melody held up her hand. "Wait a minute," she said. "Mr. Bigg is just a big guy who likes to dig up gardens. It's his job. Besides, ogres don't hunt Easter eggs. They'd squash them too easily."

Howie laughed. "Maybe he likes egg salad."

"What if he *is* a big ogre?" Liza asked. "Who else would be afraid of a little bitty kitty cat?"

Melody shrugged. She didn't know what to say. She was sure Mr. Bigg wasn't an ogre, but she couldn't prove it.

Eddie reached into the trash can and pulled out a handful of dirty eggs. "Mr. Bigg is an ogre who is trying to rid the park of people so he can have it all for himself. We have to figure out how to get rid of *him* before the Spring Festival!"

9

Friendly Change

"Wait a minute," Liza said. "Maybe we've got it all wrong."

"Me? Wrong?" Eddie sputtered. "That's not possible!"

"It wouldn't be the first time," Howie pointed out.

Liza stepped between Eddie and Howie. "I meant we're ALL wrong," she said. "Instead of getting rid of Mr. Bigg, we should help him."

"Have your brains turned into marshmallow bunnies?" Eddie blurted out. "Why should we help an ogre take over our park?"

"Eddie has a good point," Melody said. "If Mr. Bigg really is an ogre, why should we help him?"

"Because," Liza said, "the lonely ogres

in Eddie's stories wouldn't change shape again because the cat made them not trust anyone. If we show Mr. Bigg that having friends can be nice, maybe he'll *want* people to start coming to the park. We can help Mr. Bigg change."

"How would we do that?" Melody asked.

"Easy," Liza told them. "We have to become Mr. Bigg's friends."

Eddie crossed his arms over his chest and shook his head. "I'm not going to be best friends with a mud-loving, egg-stealing, cat-hating ogre," he said, "and that's final."

"Then you can stand here in the rain all by yourself," Liza said. "Because we're going to keep Mr. Bigg company. Right?" Liza looked at Melody and Howie.

"Being friendly with a lonely person doesn't sound like a bad idea," Melody said.

Howie nodded. "I say we try Liza's plan."

"Then it's decided," Liza said. "Mr. Bigg is in for a friendly change." She marched back around the piles of stone. The kids wove around puddles and hopped over mud — all except Eddie, that is. Eddie stomped in the puddles and kicked through the mud. They found Mr. Bigg at the covered picnic shelter. Liza paused for a moment to catch her breath. Then she marched right up to the giant gardener and smiled.

"This park is the loneliest place in Bailey City when it rains," she told him.

Mr. Bigg glared down at the four kids. He scratched the stubble on his chin and shrugged. "Don't mind the quiet," he said.

"But it's too quiet," Howie said. "Besides, there's nothing for us to do because of all the rain."

"So we decided we'd keep you company until the rain stops," Melody said.

Mr. Bigg frowned. "No need for that," he said. "You kiddies just run along."

"Oh, we'd much rather spend the after-

noon with you," Liza said. "We can tell you stories. Have you ever heard the story of the princess and the pea? It's a very sweet story about a little girl who couldn't sleep. That's because a tiny little pea was buried way under her pile of mattresses."

Mr. Bigg towered over Liza. "I know a few stories where little kiddies couldn't sleep, too," he growled. "But it had nothing to do with a pea. It was because hairy monsters were napping with the dust bunnies under their beds!"

Liza gasped. "There are no such things as monsters that live under beds," she told him, her voice shaking.

"Are you sure? Are you *really* sure?" Mr. Bigg asked, rubbing the stone on his ring. Instantly the rain fell harder, pounding the roof of the picnic shelter.

10

Cat City

Liza, Melody, Howie, and Eddie stood at the entrance to the park the next day. Rain drummed down on their umbrellas as they stared at the mountain of rocks blocking their way.

"It's even worse than yesterday," Liza said. "There's no way the park will be ready for the Spring Festival."

"The Easter egg hunt will be canceled," Melody said sadly.

"There won't be any golden egg this year," Howie added.

Eddie gripped the umbrella handle so hard his knuckles turned white. "There has to be an egg hunt," he muttered, "so I can win the grand prize."

"Nobody is going to win that prize,"

Melody said. "Not as long as Mr. Bigg is around."

"We can't give up. The whole city is depending on us," Eddie said.

"We tried being his friends and that didn't work," Liza pointed out. "What else can we do?"

Melody looked at Eddie. "Think. Did that library book say anything about how to get rid of ogres?"

Eddie shook his head. "Not unless you know where to find a tricky cat wearing boots," he said.

Liza gasped. "That's it!" she said, twirling around and splashing Eddie, Melody, and Howie with water from her umbrella. "Eddie is a genius!" she sang.

Eddie stood up tall and straight, smiling at his friends. "Of course I am," he said. Then his shoulders slumped a little and he scratched his head. "Um. What was my brilliant idea, anyway?"

"It's really very simple," she said. "This is all we have to do." Liza pulled her three friends close and whispered her plan to them.

"It just might work," Howie said when she finished. "But do you think there's enough time?"

"We'll have to split up and go different ways," Melody said.

"Then let's do it," Eddie said. "Meet back here just before dark."

The kids scattered in four different directions. They ran up and down streets, pounding on the doors of all the kids they knew.

Just as the clouds were turning darker with night, they headed back to the park. Only this time, they weren't alone.

Kids marched toward the park from every direction. Every one of them carried a cat and an umbrella. There were black cats, gray cats, orange cats, and striped cats. There were big cats, little cats, sleepy cats, and playful cats.

Soon there were cats here, cats there, cats and kittens everywhere.

Mr. Bigg stood in front of the mountain of stones blocking the park's entrance. His gray eyes widened when he saw what the kids were carrying.

"Where did they all come from?" Mr. Bigg bellowed.

Liza stopped right in front of Mr. Bigg and smiled her sweetest smile. "Didn't you know?" she asked. "Bailey City is a cat city!"

Mr. Bigg's eyes grew bigger and bigger as the kids with their cats and kittens came closer and closer. Suddenly, the giant gardener turned and ran, screaming across the muddy lawn as lightning flashed all around him.

11

The Golden Egg

"The sun will come out tomorrow," Melody sang at the top of her lungs. She was so happy. It was the day of the Easter egg hunt and the sun was shining brightly.

"Who cares about tomorrow?" Eddie asked. "Today is what's important. I'm ready to find that golden egg."

The kids ran down the sidewalk to the park with their Easter baskets on their arms. Workers from the Gibson Lawn and Garden Company were planting flowers near the entrance.

"Look," Liza gasped. "It's beautiful." Howie nodded. The park looked fantastic. Blooming tulips and yellow daffodils were everywhere. Green grass bordered gleaming sidewalks. A statue of a mermaid stood in the center of a fountain.

"It looks like a picture from a magazine," Melody agreed.

Eddie didn't care much about beauty, but he did care about prizes. "Come on," he said. "It's almost time for the hunt. I have to find out what's in the golden egg."

The kids had to wait for the three- to six-year-olds to finish their hunt. Eddie jumped up and down. He could hardly stand it.

Finally, the Mayor made the announcement that Eddie had been waiting for. "Seven- to ten-year-olds may line up."

"This is it," Eddie said.

Liza had a queasy feeling in the pit of her stomach. She dreaded the minute that everyone would rush to find the eggs. Everyone was always so fast they usually never left any eggs for her.

"Go!" shouted the Mayor. Liza closed her eyes as kids screamed and rushed past her. Finally, Liza opened her eyes and stepped forward. Her foot kicked a rock. But when Liza looked down, she couldn't believe her eyes. She hadn't kicked a rock at all — hidden in a clump of grass was the golden egg!

Liza closed her hand over the egg and held it tight. Her heart beat wildly. She was so thrilled she didn't even look for the other eggs filled with candy.

Melody came up to her with a basket full of eggs. "Oh, Liza," Melody said. "Didn't you find any eggs?"

Liza couldn't talk. She was too excited. "Don't worry," Melody told Liza. "I'll share my candy with you."

"Thanks," Liza managed to say. "You'll never guess what I fou —"

The Mayor interrupted Liza. "Do we have a winner?" the Mayor asked over a loudspeaker.

Melody looked around. Maybe Howie or Eddie had found the golden egg. Melody was totally surprised when Liza squeaked, "I found it!"

Howie, Melody, and Eddie stood with their mouths wide-open as the Mayor handed Liza a poster-sized certificate. It was for a trip for six to Water World.

When Liza walked over to her friends, Melody patted Liza on the back. "Way to go," Melody said.

"Congratulations," Howie told Liza.

Eddie frowned. He had really wanted to find that egg. "I hope you have a good time at Water World," Eddie said sadly.

"I hope you do, too," Liza said.

"What are you talking about?" Eddie asked. "*You* won the prize. *You* found the golden egg."

"I'm sharing my prize with you," Liza said, smiling. "After all, that's what friends are for."

Eddie jumped up and down. "I'm going to Water World!" he shouted.

Howie and Melody laughed. "I think Eddie found a prize after all," Howie said.

Melody nodded. "The best prize of all . . . friendship."

Super Spring Puzzles and Activities!

Easter Egg Hunt

The Bailey School Kids are going on an Easter egg hunt. Mr. Bigg has hidden Easter eggs in the picture on page 27. How many eggs can you find?

Answer on page 78.

Have your own Easter egg hunt!

Ask your parents or a friend to hide plastic Easter eggs all over the house or backyard. Then get  your friends together and see who can find the most eggs. For extra fun, hide a surprise like a poem, gum, or small toy inside one of the eggs.

Messy Muddy Maze

The Bailey School Kids are racing to find the golden egg. But Mr. Bigg has made a mess in the park. Can you help the kids get through the pit-falls and puddles to find the golden egg?

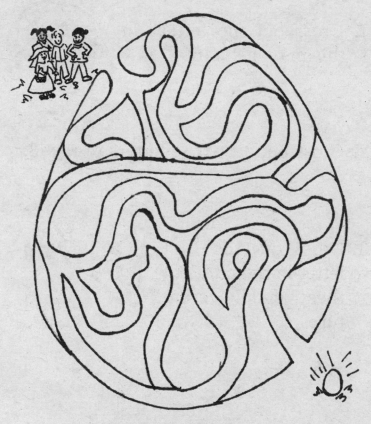

Answer on page 77.

The Golden Grid

Now that you have read *Ogres Don't Hunt Easter Eggs*, can you name one thing that ogres love? Need some help? Follow the instructions to cross out letters in the grid. The leftover letters will spell out the answer!

1. Cross out the letters in this person's name.

2. Cross out all of the letters in row 3.

3. Cross out the first letter in the name of these cuddly creatures.

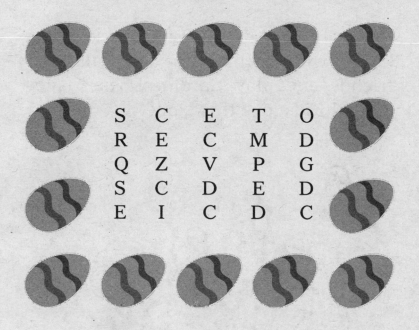

```
S   C   E   T   O
R   E   C   M   O D G
Q   Z   V   P   D G
S   C   D   E   D C
E   I   C   D   C
```

— — — — — —

Answer on page 77.

Rain, Rain, Go Away!

Is it a rainy day? Are you stuck in the house with nothing to do? Call your friends and play Sardines! The Bailey School Kids love this game.

Sardines is kind of like hide-and-seek, except that only one person hides at the beginning of the game. Here's how it works:

Pick one person to be "It." The rest of the players count to ten while the person who is "It" hides. Then the players split up to look for the person who is hiding. When a player finds "It," he or she crams into the hiding spot with "It." By the end of the game, all of the players should be squished into the same small space like a can of sardines! The last person to find the hiding spot is "It" in the next round of the game.

 If the sun comes out, you can play this game in the park or in your backyard!

Egg-cellent Rainy Day Fun

Using a sheet of paper and a pencil, trace the egg shape on the next page. Then cut out the shape and design your own Easter egg! Color your egg. Cut out shapes to paste on your egg. Add glitter, stickers, or stamps. It's your design — have fun with it!

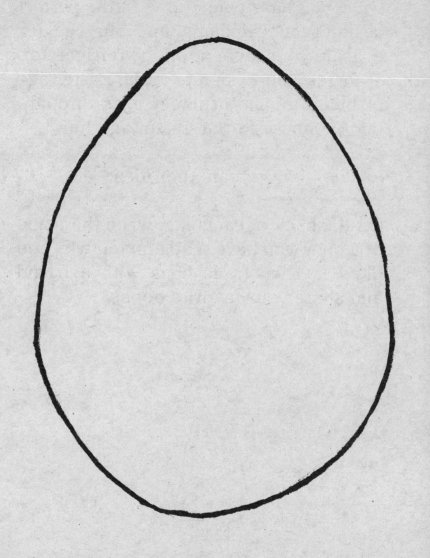

Once you have come up with the perfect design, you can hang up your egg (or eggs) in your room or on the refrigerator. Transfer your design to a real Easter egg or hide a bunch of paper eggs throughout the house for an Easter egg hunt!

Here's another idea:

On the back of each egg, write the name of a book you have read and tell why you liked it. Then trade eggs with a friend and share your favorite books!

Once Upon a Time

Here is a fun game that you can play almost anywhere. All you need are a few friends and a little bit of imagination!

Sit in a circle. One person starts a story. After a few sentences, the next person continues the story. Go around the circle a few times and see what kind of story you and your friends come up with. Or write your own story using the ideas on the next page. It can be spooky, exciting, funny, or silly!

Here are two ideas to get you started:

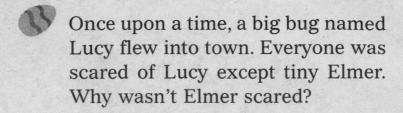 Once upon a time, a big bug named Lucy flew into town. Everyone was scared of Lucy except tiny Elmer. Why wasn't Elmer scared?

One spring, instead of rain, there was a storm of chocolate pudding. Bailey City was in a terrible fix. Could anyone save them?

Puzzle Answers

Messy Muddy Maze
page 67

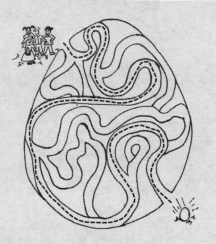

The Golden Grid
page 69

S	C̶	E̶	T	O
R	E̶	C̶	M	D̶
Q̶	Z̶	V̶	P̶	G̶
S	C̶	D̶	E̶	D̶
E̶	I̶	C̶	D̶	C̶

S T O R M S

Debbie Dadey and Marcia Thornton Jones have fun writing stories together. When they both worked at an elementary school in Lexington, Kentucky, Debbie was the school librarian and Marcia was a teacher. During their lunch break in the school cafeteria, they came up with the idea of the Bailey School Kids.

Recently Debbie and her family moved to Fort Collins, Colorado. Marcia and her husband still live in Kentucky, where she continues to teach. How do these authors write together? They talk on the phone and use computers and fax machines!

Learn more about Debbie and Marcia at their Web site, www.BaileyKids.com!

Ready for some spooky fun? Then check out this brand-new series from best-selling authors, Marcia Thornton Jones and Debbie Dadey!

Ghostville Elementary

The basement of Sleepy Hollow's elementary school is haunted. At least that's what everyone says. But no one has ever gone downstairs to prove it. Until now . . .

This year, Cassidy and Jeff's classroom is in the basement. But the kids aren't scared. There's no such thing as ghosts, right?

Tell that to the ghosts.

The basement belongs to another class — a *ghost* class. They don't want to share. And they will haunt Cassidy and her friends until they get their room back!

#1
Ghost Class

Cassidy stumbled over to the wall and flipped on the light switch. She spun around to see a boy about her age, sitting in her desk. He had dark hair that stuck up on top. He wore denim overalls and a striped shirt with a collar. She stared at his tattered shoes until his laughter made her look into his brown eyes.

"How did you do that?" Cassidy asked the boy, but he wouldn't stop laughing. "That wasn't funny at all," she told him.

She stepped toward the desk. "You'd better quit laughing," she warned. She reached over to grab him, but her hand closed around nothing except air — very cold air.

Cassidy's mouth dropped open as she hugged her own dusty arms. She had never felt such a chill. For the first time, Cassidy noticed that the boy wasn't normal. He shimmered around the edges. He was so pale that Cassidy could see right through him. He reminded her of a glowing green-frosted bubble. The boy stood up from the desk and in that instant, he disappeared.

"Where did you go?" Cassidy asked. "Come back here."

The room was still except for a whisper. "I'm warning you. Leave my desk alone."

At first, Cassidy was scared. Had she really seen a ghost? Then Cassidy got mad.

Dust covered every surface of the classroom. Mr. Morton would think she did it. "Come back here and clean up this mess!" Cassidy stomped her foot, sending a little dust cloud into the air above her sneakers. She may as well have been talking to the wind, because the boy didn't reappear.

"This is just great," Cassidy snapped. "Some kids get pen pals — I get a ghost bully."

Suddenly, a noise made Cassidy freeze. Maybe the ghost was back! She whirled around. Jeff and Nina stood at the door to the playground.

"Did you guys see that?" Cassidy asked.

"See what?" Jeff and Nina said together.

"The ghost boy," Cassidy told them.

Jeff laughed. "Yeah, right. I think I just saw a ghost boy skateboarding around the playground."

Nina put her hand on Jeff's shoulder. "I think she's serious. Cassidy really saw something."

"I'm serious, too." Jeff said with a grin. "Serious about the trouble Cassidy's going to be in when Mr. Morton sees this mess. Maybe the Ghostville ghost can help you blast this mess away," he teased.

Cassidy glared at Jeff as she stomped to the back of the room to grab a mop. "I'm not joking," she said. "I just saw a ghost right here in this very classroom."

Jeff tossed a dust mop to Cassidy. "Next you'll think that mop is a dancing skeleton."

"It's not fair," Cassidy mumbled as she swished the mop across the floor. "Not fair. Not fair. Some ghost made the mess and I have to clean it up. Not fair. Not fair. Not fair."

Cassidy stomped on the mat by the back door extra hard. She was so mad she didn't notice that something weird was happening — the little rug underneath her feet was bunching up all on its own. It wiggled, it squirmed, it bubbled, it scrunched. Suddenly, Cassidy teetered. Then she fell down right on the seat of her pants.

From somewhere in the empty basement came the sound of laughter. . . .

Creepy, weird, wacky, and
funny things happen to
the Bailey School Kids!™
Collect and read them all!

The Adventures of
THE BAILEY SCHOOL KIDS®

The Adventures of THE BAILEY SCHOOL KIDS ®

❑ BSK 0-439-04398-0 #38 Ninjas Don't Bake Pumpkin Pie ....$3.99 US
❑ BSK 0-439-04399-9 #39 Dracula Doesn't Rock and Roll ....$3.99 US
❑ BSK 0-439-04401-4 #40 Sea Monsters Don't Ride Motorcycles ....$3.99 US
❑ BSK 0-439-04400-6 #41 The Bride of Frankenstein Doesn't
                          Bake Cookies ....$3.99 US
❑ BSK 0-439-21582-X #42 Robots Don't Catch Chicken Pox ....$3.99 US
❑ BSK 0-439-21583-8 #43 Vikings Don't Wear Wrestling Belts ....$3.99 US
❑ BSK 0-439-21584-6 #44 Ghosts Don't Rope Wild Horses ....$3.99 US
❑ BSK 0-439-36803-0 #45 Wizards Don't Wear Graduation Gowns ....$3.99 US
❑ BSK 0-439-36805-7 #46 Sea Serpents Don't Juggle Water Balloons .....$3.99 US

❑ BSK 0-439-04396-4   Bailey School Kids Super Special #4:
                         Mrs. Jeepers in Outer Space ....$3.99 US
❑ BSK 0-439-21585-4   Bailey School Kids Super Special #5:
                         Mrs. Jeepers' Monster Class Trip ....$3.99 US
❑ BSK 0-439-30641-8   Bailey School Kids Super Special #6:
                         Mrs. Jeepers On Vampire Island ....$3.99 US
❑ BSK 0-439-40831-8   Bailey School Kids Holiday Special:
                         Aliens Don't Carve Jack-o'-lanterns ....$3.99 US
❑ BSK 0-439-40832-6   Bailey School Kids Holiday Special:
                         Mrs. Claus Doesn't Climb Telephone Poles .....$3.99 US
❑ BSK 0-439-33338-5   Bailey School Kids Thanksgiving Special:
                         Swampmonsters Don't Chase Wild Turkeys ......$3.99 US

Available wherever you buy books, or use this order form

Scholastic Inc., P.O. Box 7502, Jefferson City, MO 65102

Please send me the books I have checked above. I am enclosing $_____ (please add $2.00 to cover shipping and handling). Send check or money order — no cash or C.O.D.s please.

Name _____

Address _____

City_____ State/Zip _____

Please allow four to six weeks for delivery. Offer good in the U.S. only. Sorry, mail orders are not available to residents of Canada. Prices subject to change.

BSK902

THE SECRETS OF DROON

A Magical Series by Tony Abbott

Under the stairs, a magical world awaits you!

- ❑ BDK 0-590-10839-5   #1: The Hidden Stairs and the Magic Carpet
- ❑ BDK 0-590-10841-7   #2: Journey to the Volcano Palace
- ❑ BDK 0-590-10840-9   #3: The Mysterious Island
- ❑ BDK 0-590-10842-5   #4: City in the Clouds
- ❑ BDK 0-590-10843-3   #5: The Great Ice Battle
- ❑ BDK 0-590-10844-1   #6: The Sleeping Giant of Goll
- ❑ BDK 0-439-18297-2   #7: Into the Land of the Lost
- ❑ BDK 0-439-18298-0   #8: The Golden Wasp
- ❑ BDK 0-439-20772-X   #9: The Tower of the Elf King
- ❑ BDK 0-439-20784-3   #10: Quest for the Queen
- ❑ BDK 0-439-20785-1   #11: The Hawk Bandits of Tarkoom
- ❑ BDK 0-439-20786-X   #12: Under the Serpent Sea
- ❑ BDK 0-439-30606-X   #13: The Mask of Maliban
- ❑ BDK 0-439-30607-8   #14: Voyage of the *Jaffa Wind*
- ❑ BDK 0-439-30608-6   #15: The Moon Scroll
- ❑ BDK 0-439-30609-4   #16: The Knights of Silversnow

$3.99 each!

Available Wherever You Buy Books or Use This Order Form

Scholastic Inc., P.O. Box 7502, Jefferson City, MO 65102

Please send me the books I have checked above. I am enclosing $_____ (please add $2.00 to cover shipping and handling). Send check or money order–no cash or C.O.D.s please.

Name_____ Birth date_____

Address_____

City_____State/Zip_____

Please allow four to six weeks for delivery. Offer good in U.S.A. only. Sorry, mail orders are not available to residents of Canada. Prices subject to change.

www.scholastic.com

■ SCHOLASTIC

SD1102

MEET
Geronimo Stilton

A MOUSE WITH A NOSE FOR GREAT STORIES

Who is Geronimo Stilton? Why, that's me! I run a newspaper, but my true passion is writing tales of adventure. Here on Mouse Island, my books are all bestsellers! What's that? You've never read one? Well, my books are full of fun. They are whisker-licking-good stories, and that's a promise!

www.scholastic.com/kids